Pop it o

Written by Suzannah Ditchburn
Photographed by Will Amlot

Collins

It is a top.

Dom pops it on.

3

It is a map.

It is a pot.

Sam pops it on.

It is a pan.

A dog.

dog tag

8

Sit! The dog sits.

Sam taps the pots.

tap tap tap

dots

The dog sits.

Tog

The dog is sad.

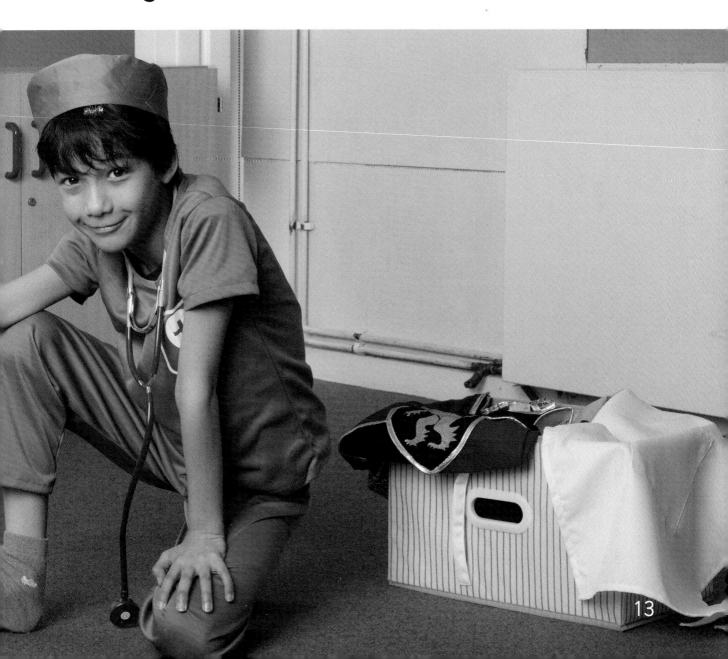

13

/g/

14

/o/

15

After reading

Letters and Sounds: Phase 2

Word count: 48

Focus phonemes: /g/ /o/

Common exception words: the, is

Curriculum links: Understanding the World; Personal, Social and Emotional Development

Early learning goals: Reading: read and understand simple sentences; use phonic knowledge to decode regular words and read them aloud accurately; read some irregular words

Developing fluency

- Your child may enjoy hearing you read the book.
- Take turns to read a page, including any labels. Encourage your child to reread the whole sentence if they hesitate over blending any sounds.

Phonic practice

- Turn to pages 2–3. Point to **pops** on page 3. Ask your child to sound out the letter in each word, then blend. (*p/o/p/s – pops*) Ensure they don't miss out the /s/ sound at the end. Ask your child to read **is** on page 2. Can they hear that the /s/ has a different sound in **is**? (/z/)
- Take turns to point out a word for the other to sound out and blend. Sound a letter out incorrectly once or twice, saying: I'm not sure that's right? Encourage your child to correct you.
- Look at the "I spy sounds" pages (14–15). Say: I can see lots of things that have the /o/ sound. Point to the fox hat and say **fox**, emphasising the /o/ sound. Ask your child to find other things that contain the /o/ sound. (*donkey, dog, blobs, octopus, pop, oranges*), Do the same for the /g/ sound. (*grapes, glasses, gift bags*)

Extending vocabulary

- Look at each double page in turn and discuss what the children have popped on. Ask your child:
  o What are they pretending to be? What clues are there in the words and pictures?